ART COULSON

THE RELUCTANT

STORYTELLER

ILLUSTRATED BY
CARLIN BEAR DON'T WALK

The Energy of the

THUNDER BEINGS

ILLUSTRATED BY
ROY BONEY JR.

&

CHEROKEE LIFE TODAY
BY TRACI SORELL

Reycraft Books
55 Fifth Avenue
New York, NY 10003

Reycraftbooks.com

Reycraft Books is a trade imprint and trademark of Newmark Learning, LLC.

Library of Congress Control Number: 2020908391

ISBN: 978-1-4788-7025-8

Printed in Dongguan, China. 8557/0620/17230

10 9 8 7 6 5 4 3 2 1

First Edition Hardcover published by Reycraft Books

Photo Credits: Front End Papers 1–3, Pages I, II, IV, 46, 60, 76, Rear End Papers 1, 2: Aunaauna/Shutterstock; Page 3: Denys Drozd/Shutterstock; Pages 10A–D, 13A, B, D, 14A, B: cstar55/Getty Images; Pages 10E, 13F: calvindexter/Getty Images; Pages 12B, E, G, H, M, 13C, E, G, H, 14C: Apostrophe/Shutterstock; Pages 12I–L: Carboxylase/Shutterstock; Page 16: Ajwad Creative/Getty Images; Page 22: EwaNew/Shutterstock; Page 36: Egor Shilov/Shutterstock; Page 47: Mountain Cubs/Shutterstock; Page 61: Eireen J/Shutterstock; Pages 62, 63A: John Elk III/Getty Images; Pages 63B, 64C, 65C: Sue Ogrocki/AP Images; Pages 64A, 65A: North Wind Picture Archives/Alamy; Pages 64B, 65B, 66B, 67B: Nativestock.com/Marilyn Angel Wynn/Alamy; Page 64D: Mike Simons/AP Images; Page 66A: Bob Pardue - Signs/Alamy; Pages 66C, 67C: John Elk/Getty Images; Page 67A: Alliance Images/Shutterstock; Page 67D: Rick & Nora Bowers/Alamy; Pages 68, 73B: Svineyard/Shutterstock; Page 69: Kelly Shannon Kelly/Alamy; Pages 70, 72C, 73A: Courtesy of Traci Sorell; Page 71: Uyvsdi/Wikimedia Commons; Page 72A: David Crenshaw/AP Images; Page 72B: chelovek/Getty Images; Page 74A: Courtesy of Art Coulson; Page 74B: Courtesy Kelly Downs Photography; Page 75: Courtesy of Carlin Bear Don't Walk

CONTENTS

ART COULSON

THE RELUCTANT

STORYTELLER

ILLUSTRATED BY
CARLIN BEAR DON'T WALK

1

THE FAMILY BUSINESS

Maurice Tenkiller came from a long line of storytellers.

Boy, could they ever talk. His mother once told him that her father, his grandfather, had talked the quills off an angry porcupine in their backyard in Oklahoma.

"That's how we got possums," she said.

Maurice's mom sure could make up stories, just like her father before her. "Have you ever seen possums running around? They really do look like porcupines without quills," she used to say. But it was her face that sold the truth. She looked so serious. She didn't even smile.

Storytelling was the Tenkiller family business, I guess you could say. Maurice's grandmother, Sally, was known throughout the Midwest for her ghost stories and tales about the old days. Maurice's uncles, Dynamite and Jack, traveled around the country telling stories at schools and events.

What? You don't know anyone who has an Uncle Dynamite? Well, Uncle Dynamite's real name was Harold. But no one ever called him that, especially once they heard him snore. Sometimes, when he napped in his chair, it sounded like a mining company was blasting the whole top off a mountain.

No one called Maurice by his given name either, except maybe his teachers on the first day of school.

Everyone knew him as Chooch, which is what his mom and dad had called him from the day he was born. They said it meant "boy" in the language his grandparents had spoken back in Oklahoma.

Chooch was a big boy. He'd gotten a growth spurt over the winter and was now nearly as tall as his uncles.

His shoulders had grown so broad that he was now wearing shirts his father and grandfather used to wear. He wore his hair long, in a single braid down his back.

The Tenkillers—Grandma, Mom, Chooch, and his uncles—lived together in a big old noisy house near Minneapolis, where they had moved years ago for work. His mom was a nurse for the Indian Health Service; his uncles were archaeologists for the Bureau of Indian Affairs.

"You heard of Indiana Jones?" his Uncle Jack had asked him more than once. "They call me Indian Jones." Hardly anyone laughed at this joke anymore.

Chooch was standing in the driveway, thinking about his uncle's corny sense of humor, when a sharp crack interrupted his thoughts. A hard rubber ball had just connected with his plastic helmet.

"You gonna catch the ball, Chooch, or stand there goofing off all day?" James Lussier waved his lacrosse stick, trying to get Chooch's attention.

"I think I'm done for the day," Chooch said, taking off his gloves and helmet. "My mom's gonna call me in for dinner any minute now."

Chooch and James were in the same class at Riverton Middle School and played for the Panthers, the traveling lacrosse team. They had lived next door to each other their whole lives.

Chooch and James—never Jim or Jimmy, always James—were inseparable. Even at night, as they slept in their neighboring houses, they were never more than one hundred feet apart. It had been this way forever.

That's what made Chooch so mad about Uncle Dynamite's plan to drag him halfway across the world to Oklahoma over spring break. Chooch was supposed to play lacrosse with James and the rest of the Panthers in the Twin Cities Native Lacrosse invitational tournament.

And to make matters even worse—if that were possible—his English teacher, Mrs. Masterson, had assigned the class a project to do over spring break: a presentation on family traditions.

It was as if the whole universe hated him.

Chooch just knew everyone expected him to talk about the "family business," storytelling.

What in the heck would he do for a whole week in Greasy, Oklahoma, population 350? They probably didn't even have Internet or TV there. And lacrosse? Forget about it.

"You'll love Greasy," Uncle Dynamite said that night, between bites of catfish and mashed potatoes. "You have thousands of cousins there—

okay, dozens of cousins," he said, correcting himself when he saw the look on Chooch's face.

They were traveling back to his family's hometown for the Wild Onion Festival, where Uncle Dynamite and Dynamite's best friend, Zeke Walkingstick, another BIA archaeologist, planned to tell stories.

"I really don't want to go. Do I have to?" Chooch pleaded with his mother and grandmother. "It's as if you all expect me to be just like you, some kind of storyteller who travels everywhere boring people to tears."

Uncle Dynamite grew quiet and looked down at his plate. His mom gave Chooch the look—you know the look, the mom look that makes someone quiet right down.

"You will enjoy yourself, whether you believe me or not," Grandma said as she started to clear the table. "There's so much to do—fishing, swimming, playing with your cousins."

"But can I play lacrosse there?"

"Even better—you can play Cherokee stickball, just like the old days," Uncle Dynamite said.

Chooch rolled his eyes.

"May I be excused? I have a lot of homework to do."

Chooch didn't really have any homework. He just wanted to get away from everyone, go up to his room, and text with James. James would understand why he was so upset.

Hi James.

They want me to be a storyteller like them. The family biz.

Chooch ended the text with an eye roll emoji. He flopped on his bed, kicked off his sneakers, and checked his phone.

11

James really understood him.

Chooch sighed.

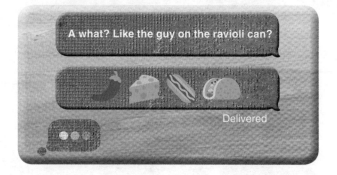

Chooch didn't even smile.

He sighed again as he tapped out a reply to his friend.

Sometimes James was a man of few words.

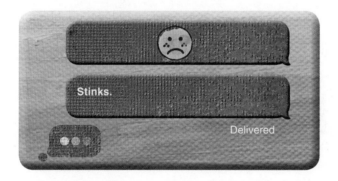

But James understood the idea of a family business. When his mom and dad had moved the family from the Red Lake reservation to the city, his dad had opened a small auto repair shop. James

worked there with his dad, his sister, and his brothers on the weekends. He planned to be a mechanic just like his dad. Or maybe work on race cars or semitrucks. A good mechanic could fix anything.

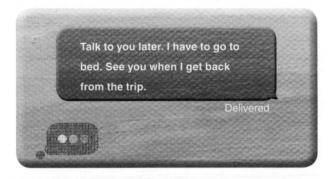

Talk to you later. I have to go to bed. See you when I get back from the trip.

Delivered

James had told Chooch many times that he wasn't sure what he'd do if he came from a family of storytellers.

Chooch plugged his phone into the family charging station in the hallway and got ready for bed.

15

2
ON THE ROAD

The next morning, the first official day of spring break, Chooch's mom woke him at dawn. She was still wearing her nurse's uniform. She had just gotten home from working overnight and wanted to say goodbye before he and Uncle Dynamite hit the road.

"Be a good boy. Tell all your cousins hi for us. And, have fun. This is a great chance for you and your uncle to spend some time together," his mom said.

Chooch sat up in his bed and rubbed the sleep from his eyes. He could barely see his mom's face in the dark room.

"I will. I will," Chooch mumbled.

Chooch was up, dressed, and downstairs in less than ten minutes. He had packed the day before— shorts, three T-shirts, jeans, and a pile of comic books his dad had given him on their last visit. They should help him pass the time.

"Grab your thermos, Dynamite, and let's go. We've got eggs and wild onions to eat!"

Chooch turned toward the familiar voice. Zeke Walkingstick, Uncle Dynamite's best friend, stood in the kitchen door.

Chooch's mom shushed him. "People are still asleep, Stick!"

Zeke was a small, muscular man, a little older than Uncle Dynamite. Although Zeke was already a short enough name, people called him Stick.

Uncle Dynamite's car was warming up in the driveway. The station wagon was a long, ugly, burnt-orange thing, rusting around the wheels. It had a faded, peeling bumper sticker that read: "Caution: Stops at All Frybread Stands."

Chooch climbed in the back seat while Dynamite and Stick threw their bags in the back.

"All set?" Uncle Dynamite asked as he slammed down the hatch.

CAUTION
STOPS AT ALL
FRYBREAD STANDS

"Yup. Oklahoma, here we come." Stick was already fastening his seat belt and putting his travel coffee mug in the drink holder.

As they made their way down Interstate 35 out of the Twin Cities, Uncle Dynamite kept looking back at Chooch in his rearview mirror.

The sun glared off the cracked windshield as the car bumped down the interstate.

Uncle Dynamite kept his left hand on the wheel and rested his right arm on the center console. The radio played softly in the background.

"Everything okay, Neph?" he asked.

"I guess." Chooch watched the farm fields glide by.

"You'll have fun. And the food sure is good back home," Uncle Dynamite said.

"That's the truth!" Stick said. "You just can't get good brown beans and corn bread up north."

Chooch smiled, in spite of himself. One day, he would bring good food to his town, food he had made himself. He loved to work in the kitchen with his mom and grandma.

Chooch liked to make up his own recipes. A few times a month, he cooked dinner for the whole family. Everyone loved his cooking.

"I just don't want to be a storyteller. That's all."

"Who said you had to be a storyteller?" Uncle Dynamite locked eyes with him in the mirror.

"It's just … I don't know. I want to do something else with my life. And you all travel everywhere, telling stories, and dragging me along. But I'm not like you."

"You don't have to be like anyone else, Chooch. You have to be only one thing in life: yourself."

STICK'S STORY

3

Stick turned around in his seat and looked back at Chooch. The lines around his mouth crinkled, and his eyes sparkled as he smiled.

"All this reminds me of a story," said Stick.

Tsula the fox didn't want to play with the other foxes. He was smaller than they were. And wrestling just wasn't his idea of fun. As the other foxes tumbled and snapped at one another down on the river bottom, Tsula stood on a nearby hill with his mother and looked up into the trees.

Tsula watched the birds flit from branch to branch and chase one another from tree to tree. More than anything, Tsula wanted to fly like the birds.

He glanced back over his shoulder and stared down his back, covered in red fur down to his pointy tail. "I wish I had a coat of feathers, like Totsuhwa the redbird," he said as he stared back up toward the top of the pines and oaks soaring above him.

"Son, why don't you go down to the river and play with your cousins?" Tsula's mother nudged him with her snout.

But instead of running down the muddy hill, Tsula darted off into the bushes. "See you later, Mother!" He smiled back at her.

As he made his way deeper into the cool forest, the birds flew down out of the trees and landed on stumps and logs all around him.

"Hey, Tsula. What are you up to?" asked Dlayvga the blue jay.

"I want to play with you and the other birds." All the birds twittered and tweeted and laughed.

"But you're a fox," Totsuhwa said, pointing out the obvious. All the birds, as if to make a point, darted up into the air, dancing and twirling as they rose higher and higher.

Tsula tried his best to follow them. He jumped in the air and waved his legs. But no matter how hard he tried, he couldn't fly.

So he ran. He chased the birds as they glided over meadows and streams. He hopped over logs and sailed down hills. He panted and grunted, but he never slowed down.

The birds began to fly up the hill we used to call Inadv Gadusi, or Snake Mountain. They climbed and climbed. Eventually, they broke through the clouds and mist. And still they rose.

As the sun went down and day turned to dusk, Tsula followed the birds, his paws barely brushing the forest floor as he ran.

When they reached the top of Snake Mountain, the birds flew loops and arcs in all directions. As they sailed out past the cliff face and over the dark valley below, Tsula never stopped. The little fox leaped toward the rising moon, out into the open air.

Tsula looked down. His heart skipped. His stomach felt funny. But he didn't fall.

He looked to his right. He looked to his left. Where once were legs and paws, he saw flat, leathery wings. He beat them as quickly as he could.

He was flying! He darted this way and that in the light of the moon.

The birds looked back and flapped toward him. Dlayvga shouted with excitement, "Tsula! You're not a fox anymore!"

And from that day forward, Tsula was known as Tlameha. And he flew with his friends, the birds, but only at night.

TSU

LA TLAMEHA

As he finished his story, Stick made his hands flap, like bird wings. Then he turned to face the road again.

"Hey, Chooch, do you know what that word means? Tlameha?" Uncle Dynamite looked back at his nephew through the mirror, his right eyebrow raised.

"Does it mean 'bird'?" Chooch asked.

Both men laughed. "Close," Stick chuckled. "Tlameha means 'bat.' And think about it. Bats fly so high, they're hard to see, especially at night. But a bat has the face of a fox. Mean-looking little things."

"Do you get the point of that story?" his uncle asked.

Chooch sat in silence, listening to the car hum beneath him. "Not really," he said at last.

Stick turned around. As he caught Chooch's eye, he said, "Well, the way I take it, it means you're never stuck being who everyone else thinks you are. With a little effort, you can become whatever you want to be."

Chooch nodded and smiled. He understood.

"That's a great story."

After twelve long hours in the car and endless stories about the people, places, and animals of Oklahoma, the three tired travelers pulled into the long gravel driveway of a home in the small town of Greasy.

As they took their bags out of the car, the porch light came on, and they found themselves surrounded by excited children and barking dogs.

"A Cherokee Nation homecoming," Stick said with a laugh. "Is that frybread I smell?"

"Yes, and some hog meat and grape dumplings," said Aunt Pearl. She was Chooch's mom and Uncle Dynamite's sister. "Hello, boys. C'mon in and take a load off."

After their dinner and a lot of excited talk and laughter, Dynamite, Stick, and Chooch grabbed their bags and said their good nights before heading to the closed-in back porch, where they would sleep.

"Busy day tomorrow. We have some lies to tell," Dynamite said, winking at his sister. "Wado. Thanks for letting us rack out here for a few days."

Aunt Pearl smiled and swatted at him. "What were we going to do? Let you sleep out in the barn with the sheep?"

The next day, the smell of bacon woke Chooch from a deep sleep.

"Don't eat too much," Uncle Dynamite told him as he gobbled down bacon, biscuits, and scrambled eggs with wild onions. "There'll be a hog fry and more wild onions at the festival today."

That afternoon, the two men and Chooch sat under the trees as a small, dark woman in a flowing blue dress told a story about a rabbit and an otter. Families listened to her, sitting anywhere there was shade.

Even though it was early spring, the day was hot and muggy. Some of the people were eating pieces of watermelon and speaking in the Cherokee language. Chooch could understand a word or two, but he didn't really know what they were saying.

Next to Stick stood an old man, leaning on his cane. He cleared his throat until Chooch looked over at him.

"You going next, Chooch? You have a story to tell us?"

Chooch shook his head. "I don't know any stories. I was just about to go over and see if the cooks needed any help." Chooch rose to his feet and made his way to the cook fires before anyone else got the bright idea that he was some kind of storyteller.

Chooch soon found himself busy with the other cooks, cutting up onions, adding sugar and eggs to cornmeal dough, and stirring the hog meat in a big iron kettle with a long wooden paddle.

One of the cooks even allowed Chooch to prepare a huge pot of pinto beans, adding his own mix of spices, herbs, vegetables, and pork bones.

After a bit, Chooch dished up a big plate of beans, hog meat, greens, and corn bread. He carried it carefully back to where he had been sitting. When he got there, he walked up to the elder who had talked with him earlier and handed him the plate.

The old man took a bite and chewed slowly. He took another bite. Then another.

"Did you make this food for us, Chooch?" the old man asked, pausing between bites.

"Yes. Does it taste okay?"

"Osdadv! It's great!" He looked over at Dynamite and Stick and nodded his approval. Chooch had made an impression.

Chooch looked down at his shoes and smiled.

"You know, son, there's more ways than one to tell a story," the elder said to Chooch.

Uncle Dynamite said, "That's right."

"You don't have to stand up in front of everyone and string a bunch of words together," the old man continued. He waved with his fork for emphasis. "Some people sing their stories. Others dance. Some even paint pictures. Each of them is a storyteller in his or her own way. Your food can tell your story."

Stick mumbled his agreement as he put another piece of corn bread in his mouth.

"What's that you're saying, Stick?" Uncle Dynamite asked, laughing.

Chooch was proud that they liked his food. He thought about the importance of food and family gatherings and, yes, even the stories that people told when they got together.

Helping to feed his family was part of a larger family tradition he had never really thought much about.

"You know, Uncle Dynamite, I think I have a great idea for my school project on family traditions."

For once in his life, Chooch couldn't wait to do his homework.

ART COULSON

THE ENERGY OF THE
THUNDER BEINGS

ILLUSTRATED BY
ROY BONEY JR.

48

Saloli peered up at the top of the mountain, still wearing its blanket of mist. His mother had warned him not to climb the mountain the Cherokee people called the Standing Man. The Thunder Beings, who brought rain to feed the crops, lived there. Saloli knew they did not like to be disturbed.

"The Little People also lived in the mountain's caves," his mother said. The Little People looked just like Cherokee people but were the size of small children. He had heard that they liked to play tricks on people and suspected it was best to avoid them, too.

"It's dangerous up there," his mother said. "You have plenty to do here on the ground, little Squirrel. You don't need to climb into the sky."

Saloli was torn. He wanted to mind his mother. But he needed to make a new pair of sticks to play the ball game, anetsodi. The strongest hickory trees in the world grew on the slopes of the Standing Man.

Plus, it was a windy day, which would make the steep climb even harder. After a few steps up, a gust knocked Saloli to the ground. He rolled back to where he started. "Osiyo, Unole! Hello, Wind! I didn't come to fight you today," Saloli said to the gust as it flew by overhead.

Another gust screamed by with laughter in its whistle. Saloli, however, pulled himself to his feet, determination his guide. "I'm coming up the mountain, anyway," he called out to the Thunder Beings and Little People. "I won't bother you. I just need some hickory to make ball sticks."

As Saloli climbed the mountain, he could hear the Thunder Beings rumble. He followed a roaring stream into a meadow cut through with a narrow path. Along the path he found a turtle-shell rattle, the kind used during ceremonial dances. He did not pick it up. Instead, he put his hands to his mouth and called out, "Little People! I am leaving this here for you. Tla yaquaduliha."

He walked on. Soon, he found a pair of tiny moccasins on the path. He did not pick them up. He called out again, "Tla yaquaduliha. I am leaving these here for you."

A third time he stopped. There was a cane basket filled with fresh berries the size of his fist. Again, he called out, "Tla yaquaduliha. I am leaving these for you."

With the force of sheer will the boy pushed upward. Near the top of the mountain, Saloli heard a loud yet beautiful, even musical, crashing sound. It reminded him of long nights watching the stomp dances at the ceremonial grounds. Gravity was the lead dancer and the cascading waterfall a thousand turtle-shell rattles. This was the home of the Thunder Beings. As Saloli drew closer, he saw a flash—a bolt of lightning! The lightning missed him but traveled straight at a nearby hickory tree. Then he heard the Thunder Beings roar. The sound was loud and forceful. Its vibrations hit him in a series of quick waves and knocked him to the ground.

Saloli turned to look at the tree, now burning from the heat of the lightning bolt. Next to the tree stood a man shorter than Saloli. He wore a deer hide tunic and a cloth turban. The Little Person spoke to Saloli in a strange form of Cherokee, but the boy understood.

"Even though that tree has been struck by lightning," the man said, "it is still alive—and much stronger than before. It will make excellent stickball sticks."

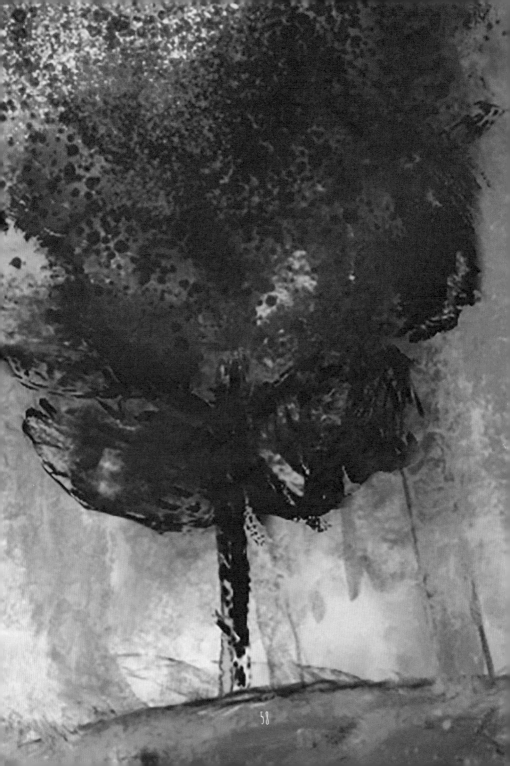

"The energy from the lightning changed the wood," he continued. "It got burnt, but it is special now. Plant some in your cornfield and the corn will grow large."

"Wado," said Saloli. "Thank you. But why are you helping me?"

"Remember those items you passed as you walked? You didn't take what wasn't yours. And you knew the right words to say," replied the man.

Saloli thanked the Little Person again and cut a pair of branches for his sticks. Then he carefully carved out the burnt wood and wrapped it in deer hide.

When he returned home, Saloli knew not to tell his mother about the Little Person or where the Thunder Beings lived.

These must always be kept secret.

TRACI SORELL

CHEROKEE

Life Today

The Cherokee Nation is located among the wooded green hills of northeastern Oklahoma. You'll find large lakes, rural towns, winding rivers, gravel roads, small cities, and some of the friendliest people you'll ever meet here. More than 370,000 citizens make up the Cherokee Nation. About 125,000 of them live within the tribe's fourteen-county jurisdictional area. The rest live in other parts of Oklahoma and all around the world.

CHEROKEE NATION

**CHEROKEE NATION
JURISDICTIONAL AREA**

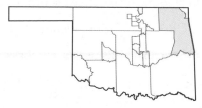

LANGUAGE

Tsalagi
[JAH-LAH-GHEE] = Cherokee

Osiyo
[OH-SEE-YO] = Hello

Osda
[OHS-dah] = Good/Great

Wado
[WAH-doe] = Thank you

YONA
[YO-nah] = Bear

Part of the Cherokee Nation's focus centers on providing its citizens access to healthcare, homes, education, and employment. The tribe has built many healthcare clinics across the fourteen-county area. This allows tribal citizens to find medical help closer to home. There are also programs that the Cherokee Nation operates to help repair homes and build new ones that tribal citizens can purchase.

In addition to providing extra funding to local schools, the tribe also operates its own pre-K through sixth-grade language-immersion school and a combined school for seventh through twelfth-grade students. Also, eligible Cherokee citizens, whether or not they live within the jurisdictional area, can apply for higher-education scholarships.

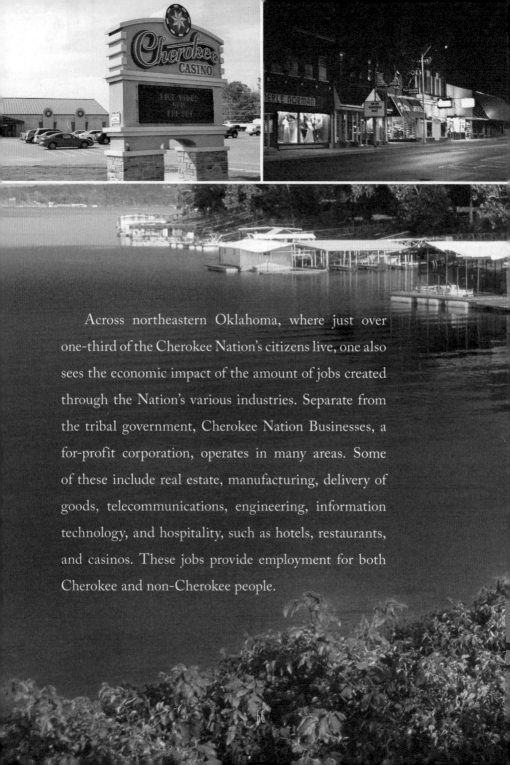

Across northeastern Oklahoma, where just over one-third of the Cherokee Nation's citizens live, one also sees the economic impact of the amount of jobs created through the Nation's various industries. Separate from the tribal government, Cherokee Nation Businesses, a for-profit corporation, operates in many areas. Some of these include real estate, manufacturing, delivery of goods, telecommunications, engineering, information technology, and hospitality, such as hotels, restaurants, and casinos. These jobs provide employment for both Cherokee and non-Cherokee people.

But some of the most important work that the tribal government does is reflected in its mission statement: "preserving and promoting Cherokee culture, language, and values." The Cherokee Nation now offers a variety of programs and services in person and online for its citizens, regardless of where they live. Each Labor Day weekend, the Cherokee Nation celebrates the signing of the 1839 constitution at its Cherokee National Holiday in Tahlequah. More than 60,000 people attend this event. If you attend, you'll be able to watch traditional game competitions, such as a cornstalk shoot and Cherokee marbles, and softball and golf tournaments. You can also enjoy storytelling, the Principal Chief's State of the Nation address, a parade, a children's fishing derby, arts and crafts, live music, a variety of Cherokee foods, and an intertribal powwow.

Throughout the year, the Cherokee Nation offers classes on traditional arts, games, and tribal history across the fourteen counties as well as in cities around the U.S., where large numbers of Cherokee citizens live. Cherokee language classes are available free online. Cherokee elders are teaching younger generations the language, the traditional games, and the arts. This allows those learning to pass on the knowledge to the next generation and keep the traditions going. The tribe honors those who have outstanding knowledge of Cherokee art forms and cultural practices and are committed to preserving or reviving them. Those Cherokee citizens chosen for this award are named Cherokee National Treasures.

Like most of you reading this book, Cherokee children attend public schools and participate in sports and other extracurricular activities. They also benefit from the tribe's ability to offer special culture and language programs beyond what is taught at home. Each summer, the Cherokee Nation offers a free weeklong overnight camp for teenage citizens in the eighth through twelfth grades focusing on science, technology, engineering, art, and math. The tribe also offers summer cultural day camps for younger citizens too. Cherokee children can also try out for the Cherokee National Youth Choir or compete to represent the tribe as Little Cherokee Ambassadors.

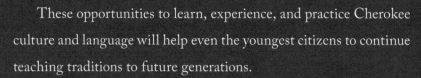

These opportunities to learn, experience, and practice Cherokee culture and language will help even the youngest citizens to continue teaching traditions to future generations.

Each spring and fall, the Cherokee Heritage Center welcomes school groups just like yours to visit and play traditional games like chunkey and stickball. You'll even learn a few words like tsalagi (JAH-lah-ghee), which means Cherokee, and yona (YO-nah), which means bear. You'll get to hear Cherokee stories, some funny and others a little spooky. If you can't make it to the Cherokee Heritage Center with your school group, you're still welcome to visit anytime!

TSALAGI

ABOUT AUTHORS

ART COULSON

Art Coulson is Cherokee and comes from a family of storytellers. He is the author of *The Creator's Game* and *Unstoppable*. Art lives in Minnesota with his family but still plays traditional Cherokee stickball when he visits friends and relatives in the Cherokee Nation of Oklahoma.

TRACI SORELL

Traci Sorell writes award-winning fiction and nonfiction books as well as poems for children. Some of her works include: *We Are Grateful: Otsaliheliga*, *At the Mountain's Base*, and *Indian No More*. Traci is an enrolled citizen of the Cherokee Nation and lives with her family in northeastern Oklahoma, where her tribe is located.

& ILLUSTRATORS

CARLIN BEAR DON'T WALK

Carlin Bear Don't Walk is an acclaimed Crow and Northern Cheyenne Artist from Busby, Montana. His award-winning art is an energetic blend of colorful oils, unique Impressionism, and surreal themes. It is collected throughout the world and can be found in many galleries, universities, museums, and private collections.

ROY BONEY JR.

DB ᎣᎮᏍ ᎠᎳᎯ Roy Boney Jr. is a full blood citizen of the ᏣᎳᎩ ᏕᎦᏲᎯ Cherokee Nation. He is an award-winning artist, writer, and filmmaker with a BFA in Graphic Design and a MA in Studio Art. His work has been shown throughout the United States and internationally. He currently works in the Language Program for Cherokee Nation Educational Services Group in Tahlequah, Oklahoma, where he lives.

FOR SALLY MILLS RACKLIFF, WHOSE STORIES
SHOWED ME A WIDER, WONDERFUL WORLD.

-ARt Coulson